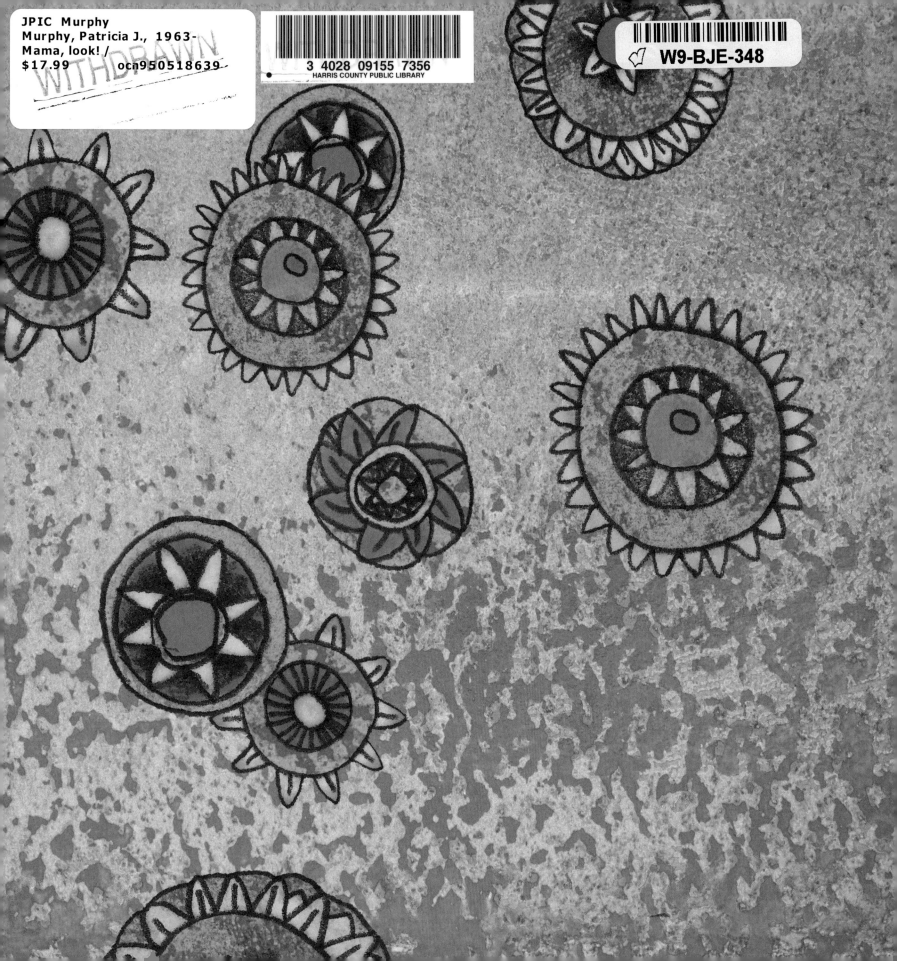

For our dear mamas,
Joanne Olive Murphy
and Ana Calderon

–P.J.M. and D.D.

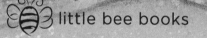

little bee books

An imprint of Bonnier Publishing USA
251 Park Avenue South, New York, NY 10010
Text copyright © 2017 by Patricia J. Murphy
Illustrations copyright © 2017 by David Diaz
Manufactured in China   LEO 1216
First Edition
2 4 6 8 10 9 7 5 3 1
Library of Congress Cataloging-in-Publication Data
is available upon request.
ISBN 978-1-4998-0080-7

littlebeebooks.com
bonnierpublishingusa.com

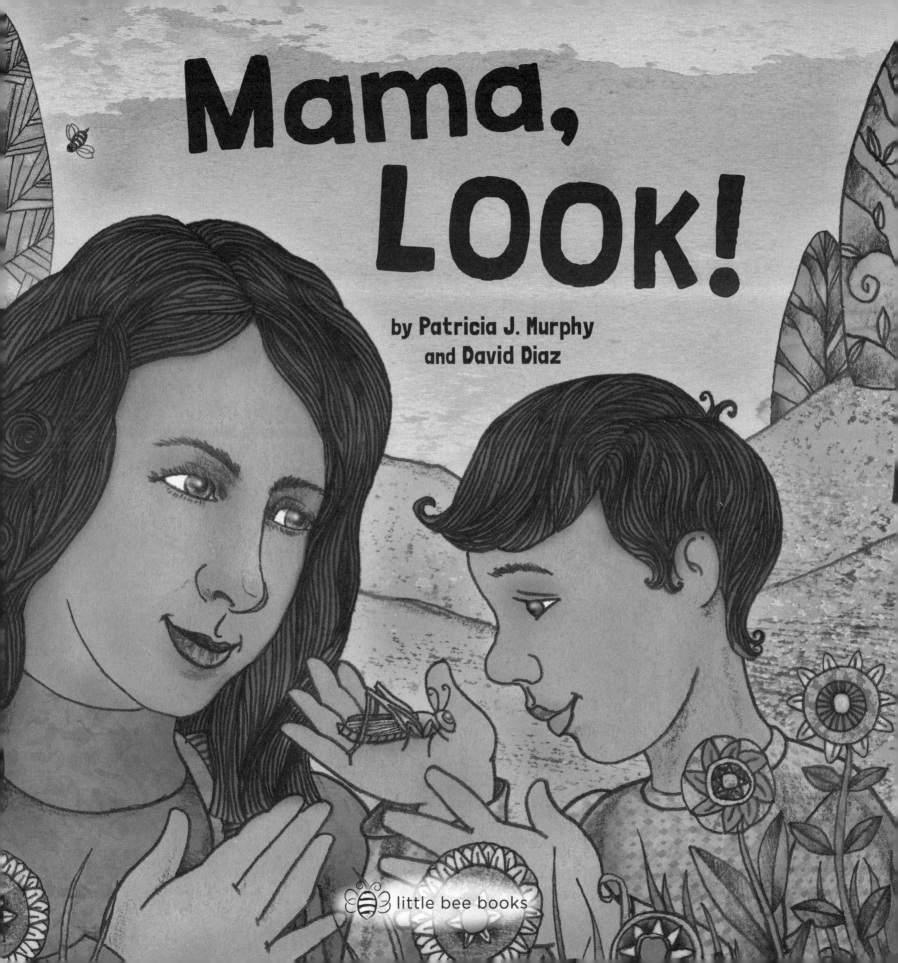

Mama, LOOK!

by **Patricia J. Murphy**
and **David Diaz**

little bee books

Grasshoppers.

Mama, LOOK!

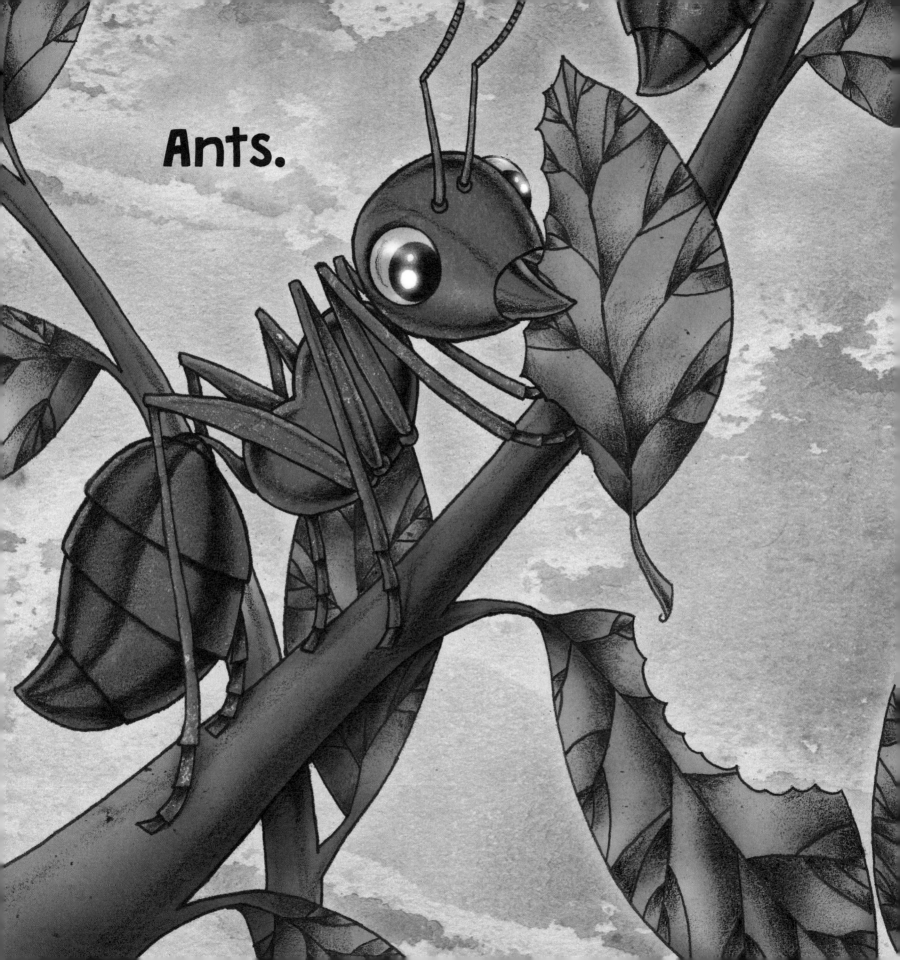

Ants.

Mama, LOOK!

Butterflies.

Frogs.

Fish.

Ducks.

Bunnies.

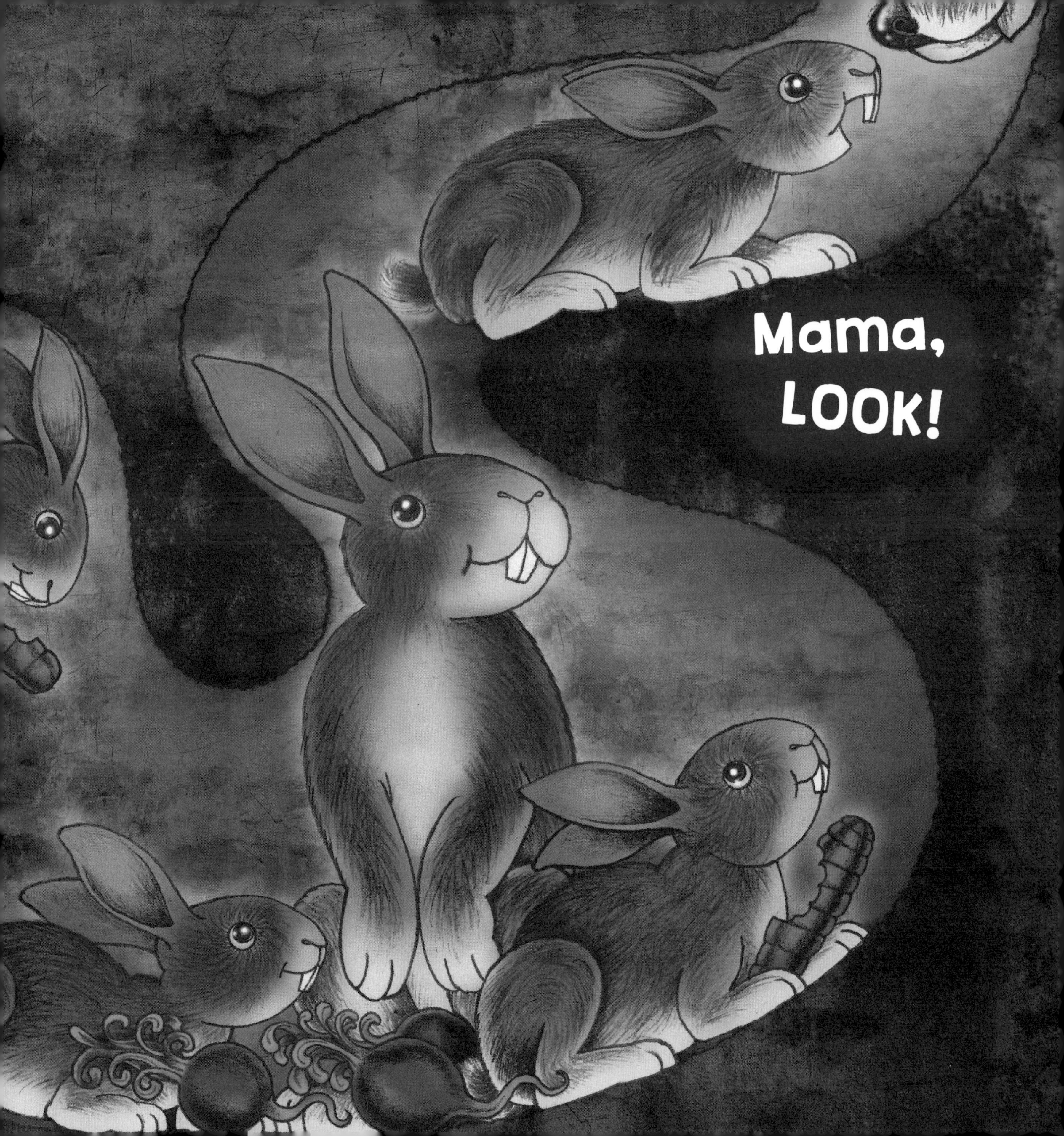
Mama,
LOOK!

Puppies.

Squirrels.

Mama,
LOOK!

Bees.

Mama, LOOK!

Baby.

Mama,
LOOK!

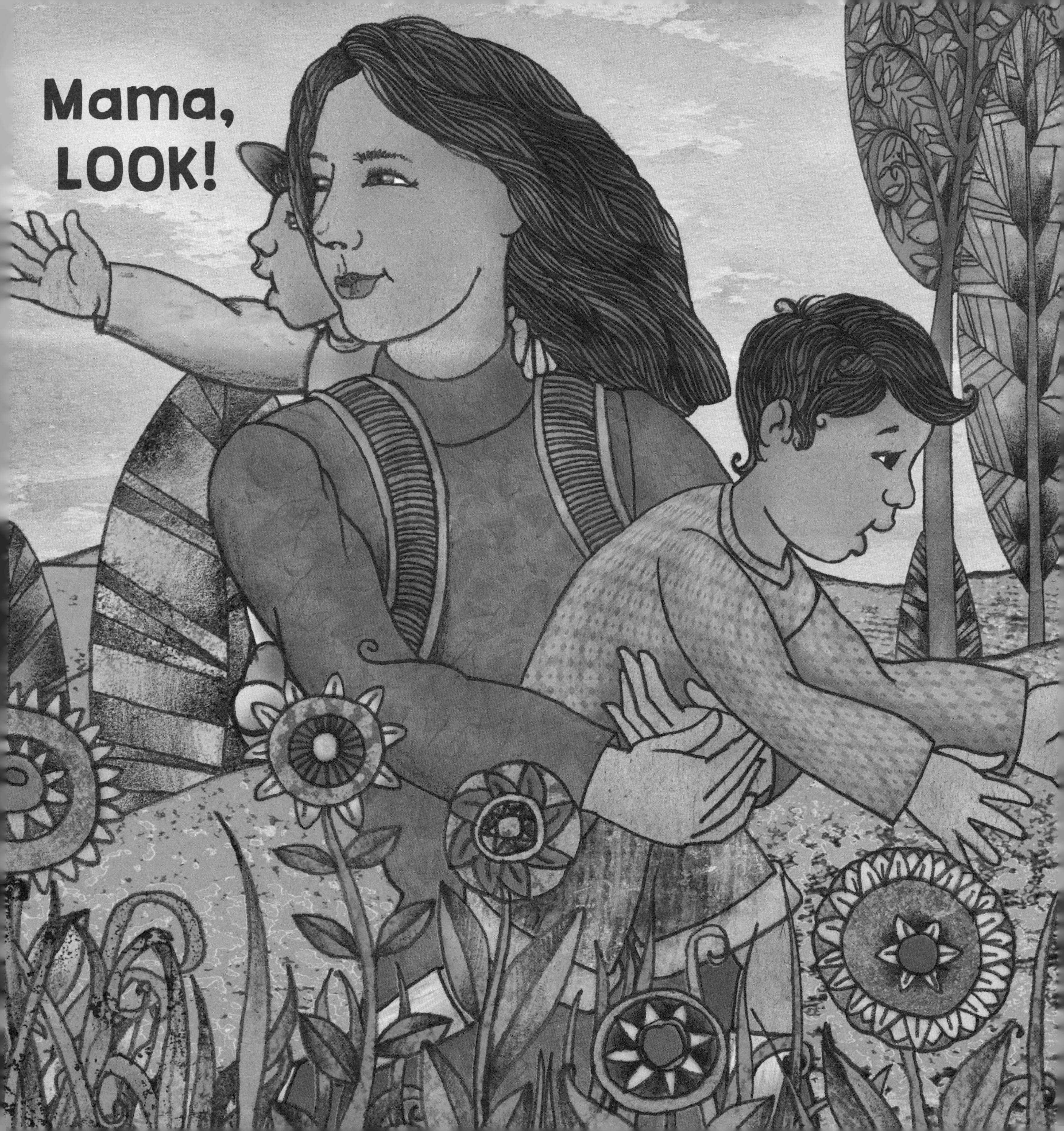

Authors' Note

It all began in a library (well, actually two libraries) where many magical things often do. Picture a young boy yelling, "Mama, LOOK!" as he spies a fish swimming by in the Arlington Heights Memorial Library KIDS' WORLD aquarium, and, then, a chance encounter between two picture book creators at a children's literacy festival at the Harold Washington Library in Chicago, and you have the beginning of a story—our story—and this story!

Created with inspiration, imagination, collaboration, divine intervention, and David's "otherworldly" illustrations, our story sets into motion a series of caring, sharing moments between mamas and babies, and honors all kinds of mamas and babies everywhere.

We dedicate this story to our dear mamas, and to YOU.

Take a "Mama, LOOK!" Walk!

Dear Mamas, Babies, and Families:

Take a "Mama, LOOK!" walk with your family members and spend some time outside in nature. Notice the animals that you see in your backyard or nearby park, on the playground, at the local zoo, or on a farm. Do you see mamas and babies? What do they look like? What sounds do they make? Do they notice you?

Observing nature lets us learn about the world around us. It is also how we came up with the animals to include in our book! While you are observing, talk about what you notice, draw or sketch what you see, take pictures, make lists, and share what you find!

Happy LOOK-ing!